This book belongs to

_____

Children's
POOLBEG

Candy on the DART

First published 1989 by
Poolbeg Press Ltd
Knocksedan House,
Swords, Co Dublin, Ireland

Reprinted August, 1991
Reprinted May 1995

ISBN 1 85371 057 1

Cover design by Pomphrey Associates
Typeset by Print-Forme,
62 Santry Close, Dublin 9.
Printed by The Guernsey Press Co Ltd,
Vale, Guernsey, Channel Islands.

Candy on the DART

Ita Daly

Children's
POOLBEG

For Sarah

Contents

Contents

1

Candy's Decision

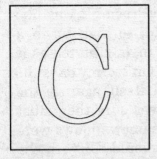andy O'Brien thought she had never been so unhappy in her life. She lay on her bed, staring at the grey wall of the garden shed and listening to the rain drumming down onto its corrugated roof. Of course, this lumpy bed wasn't hers, anymore than the room with the dismal view was. Her real bedroom was up in the attic, under the eaves and looking out over the sea to Ireland's Eye.

"Please, Mammy," she had said when she was nine. "Can I move up to the attic now? I want to be nearer the wind and the sea birds and I want to be able to look down on the sea."

"But you might be lonely up there."

"Not at nine."

So the attic walls had been painted white, and pink curtains made for its windows.

Candy's bed had been positioned under a skylight so that she went to sleep at night watching the stars in winter and birds swooping past as the evenings lengthened.

Candy loved her attic bedroom. It was like being in a different world, so high up in a house which was already high, situated as it was on the Hill of Howth. On stormy days the wind howled and hurled itself against the windows so that Candy was sure they must break. In summer, those same windows were flung open and the attic would fill with the smell of wild flowers. If she did get lonely or feel frightened, all she had to do was cuddle up to Pangur Bán. He was an old cat now and he had given up his night wanderings. He loved to curl up on Candy's duvet and before settling down to sleep he would lick her face.

Now Pangur was in the boarding kennels in Howth and Candy was in this miserable boxroom.

And all because of Mrs Nolan.

"You'll love her," Candy's mother had said. "Auntie Caroline says that she was by far the sweetest nanny they ever had." Auntie Caroline was not a blood relation. She was a very posh lady who had married Uncle Christopher and who had been brought up in a castle in Co. Meath surrounded by maids and governesses and nannies. She was forever offering advice to Candy's mother and telling her what to do. Candy considered her a busybody.

"But why do I have to stay at home anyway?" Candy wanted to know. "Why can't I come to Nepal with Daddy and you? I'd like to discover a Yeti—it'd be far better for my education than staying here with Mrs Nolan and going to boring old school."

"Now Candy, don't be silly, we've already discussed this. You must stay here and be good and we'll phone you as soon as we get there. We'll write as often as we can and I'm sure you'll have a great time with Mrs Nolan."

Candy loved her parents dearly but she had often wished that they were not quite so clever. Less clever parents might have had more ordinary jobs and more time to spend at home with their children. Her friends at school often said they envied Candy such clever parents who seemed to lead such interesting lives and were interviewed on television about their work. Candy *was* proud of them but she just wished—she just wished that they had left her with someone other than Mrs Nolan.

What an actress that woman was though. How successfully she had fooled everybody.

"Don't you worry about a thing, Mrs O'Brien," she had said as Mammy had been explaining to her what a faddy eater Candy was. "Candy and I are going to get on just fine. I really love children, although I've never been lucky enough to have had any of my own." Her blue eyes had smiled wistfully and her white curls had bobbed innocently. "I consider it a privilege to be allowed look after Candy while you and your husband are abroad on your important work."

Candy had been fooled, too, and it wasn't until the telephone call had come to tell her that her parents had arrived safely in Nepal that Mrs Nolan had come out in her true colours.

"It's time you were in bed," she had said as Candy was putting down the phone.

"But it's only eight o'clock and I never ... "

"Don't you dare argue with me," Mrs Nolan had screamed. "You may have twisted your parents round your little finger but I'm boss now. Bed I said."

Next morning Candy was greeted by Mrs Nolan standing at the bottom of the stairs and pointing at her watch.

"I said breakfast was at eight o'clock, not two minutes past. And what sort of a silly name is Candy? I can't call you that — haven't you got another?"

"My name is really Candida."

"Hmph — that's nearly as bad, but I suppose it'll have to do. Well, Candida, if you're late again for meals, you won't get any food. That'll soon cure your faddy eating habits."

Candy soon discovered that Mrs Nolan was a very moody person. She flew into rages for no reason; then sometimes, when Candy came back from school, she could be quite jolly, offering to share her bag of smoky bacon crisps. Most of the time she was just quietly bad-tempered and Candy learned to stay out of her way. She noticed, too, that as time went by there seemed to be less and less food in the house. Mrs Nolan didn't buy cakes or biscuits and neither did she bake them. She didn't buy fruit either or sausages or ice-cream and she and Candy lived for the most part on what she described as "good, nourishing Irish stew." This consisted of tough gristly chunks of meat in a watery gravy, with bits of potato floating around if they were lucky.

What mystified Candy was the fact that

Mrs Nolan and her shopping trolley were forever taking trips to the supermarket and when she returned to the house the trolley was full of *something*, or so it seemed from the way that she was dragging it along behind her.

One night, Candy found an answer to the housekeeper's peculiar behaviour. She had come down to the kitchen to get her schoolbag, having remembered some Irish spellings that had yet to be learned. As she approached the kitchen door she heard singing and, as she peeped round the door, she found Mrs Nolan sprawled over the table, a full tumbler and an empty gin bottle in front of her. Before she could back out, Mrs Nolan had seen her. Her singing stopped abruptly and she offered Candy a sickly smile.

"Come in and sit down. I'm just having a little drink for this terrible toothache."

"I don't think gin and tonic is very good for that, Mrs Nolan ... "

Candy had meant to add that she thought hot whiskey would be better — she remembered her Cork granny using it with great relief — but she had no time to say any more for, staggering up from the table, Mrs Nolan had grabbed her by the shoulder.

"So you dare to criticize your elders and betters — do you? I can see how badly brought up you are. You need the stick and no mistake."

Twisting free, Candy had fled from the kitchen, up to her bedroom. At first she listened for Mrs Nolan's footsteps, but when these did not materialize she eventually went to bed.

Next morning the housekeeper greeted her pleasantly enough, making no reference to the night before. As she was finishing her breakfast, Mrs Nolan, smiling nastily at her, said, "I'm afraid, Candida dear, I cannot have you sleeping up at the top of the house. I'm responsible for you and I want you down here beside me. You can move into the box-room when you come home from school."

"Please, Mrs Nolan, please don't make me leave my room."

"I'm sorry, child, but I couldn't rescue you up there if a fire broke out — I couldn't climb all those stairs. And — Candida."

"Yes?"

"You'll have to put that cat of yours away somewhere. I can't have it here, it's bringing on my asthma. I'd forgotten I was allergic to cats."

Candy didn't believe this for a second. She knew that Mrs Nolan was doing all this to punish her because she had found her drunk in the kitchen. She also knew that there was nobody to turn to. With her parents away, whom could she complain to? Anyway, what grown-up would believe her when they looked into Mrs Nolan's kindly face and twinkling blue eyes? They would dismiss her as a wicked, ungrateful girl, making up stories.

Candy had thought that life couldn't get any worse, but today at school she had discovered otherwise. It was when she had had the row with Siobhán Murtagh that she decided she was not going to put up with things any longer.

Siobhán Murtagh was supposed to be her best friend, someone she could turn to for sympathy when things were going badly. As they sat eating their lunch side-by-side, she had said, without thinking, "I hope I get a phone call from Mammy and Daddy tonight."

Siobhán Murtagh had continued licking the lid of her yoghurt carton. Then she said in a scornful voice, "Oh do stop going on about your parents — I'm really fed up hearing about them. All we hear all day long is about Nepal and the Himalayas and the Yeti. You should stop boasting, Candy."

Candy had found it difficult to keep her tears back. Maybe she had been going on a bit about her parents but it was only because she was missing them so much. She had expected Siobhán to understand that, Siobhán who had a brother and sister as well as a mother and father.

She had said nothing, but it was then that she had decided to run away. She would leave the lot behind—school, Mrs Nolan and Siobhán Murtagh, and try her luck in the wide world beyond. It couldn't be any worse than the one she was leaving.

2

Running Away

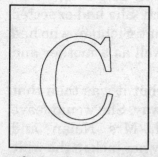

andy took her books from her school bag and placed them in a neat pile in the bottom of her wardrobe. Then she put some clean knickers, socks, jeans and a jumper in the bag and stuffed them down. She still had to fit in her old doll, Linda, for even at ten she couldn't leave home without her. She took her savings—£10—from her moneybox and put it in the outside pocket of the bag. Grabbing a toothbrush and comb from the bathroom, she was set for the road.

In the kitchen, Mrs Nolan paid her little attention. She sat hunched over the breakfast table, muttering to herself as she drank her tea.

Candy ate up her lumpy porridge and burnt toast and quietly took the dishes over to the sink.

"I'll make my own lunch, Mrs Nolan," she said. "Why don't you go back to bed for a while? I can see that you've got one of your headaches."

Mrs Nolan glared at her, then smiled unconvincingly. "I think I will then. I've a busy day ahead of me—the washing and the grass and the brasses. This is a big house and a terrible responsibility for one lone woman. No wonder I'm getting headaches."

There was not much in the fridge, but in a cupboard Candy discovered two packets of crisps and a jar of olives. She distributed these among her blazer pockets and made a cheese sandwich with what was left of the bread.

"Good-bye Mrs Nolan," she called and, banging the door after her, she walked down the path without a backward glance.

It was a lovely May morning. The sun was already up and the world was without shadows. Candy turned away from her usual path to school and began the descent towards the DART station.

DART stood for Dublin Area Rapid Transport and Candy loved the system with its bright, clean trains. She had decided that she would use it as a means of escape, taking the train to a certain station and then changing to another. She had seen people do this in films and she thought that if Mrs Nolan bothered to come looking for her, this route would put her off the scent. Candy didn't know where her journey would take her and now she didn't much care. She was beginning to see this as the start of a great adventure.

She approached the ticket office. "A half fare into town please."

"Look, love, it's no use handing me that ten pound note at this hour of the morning. Have you nothing smaller?"

"No, I'm sorry."

"Then you'll just have to wait. Stand over there."

"That's all right," a man's voice interrupted, coming from behind her shoulder. "I'll get that fare."

Candy felt she was going to get sick. She had recognised the voice, that of Stuart Hartigan's father. The Hartigans lived just around the corner from the O'Briens. Any minute now Mr Hartigan would be asking her had she got the day off from school and, if so, why she was wearing her school uniform.

But he was smiling down at her. "How are your parents, Candy? Keeping well?"

Before she could answer he was handing

her her ticket and walking away. "You don't mind if I don't sit with you? There's something in here," he pointed to his briefcase, "that I just have to read before I get to work. Good-bye Candy ... enjoy yourself."

Not for the first time Candy wondered how grown-ups managed to run the world. Their crankiness was only surpassed by their vagueness and unpredictability. However, on this occasion she was grateful for Mr Hartigan's preoccupation. She doubted that after a day in the office he would even remember that he had seen her this morning. Quickly she slipped into the waiting train and sat down by the window. The carriage began to fill up and soon she could no longer see Mr Hartigan. She listened with envy to two schoolboys opposite discuss whose mother was going to pick them up after the match but then she told herself that she was really better off— this was a proper adventure that she was embarking on.

At Kilbarrack she got off. She knew nothing about this area other than the sign on the station platform. She waited until the train had left the station and then began to walk towards the exit.

Outside, a vast housing estate began its

sprawl. Candy placed her schoolbag on the ground and took out a packet of crisps. She knew she would have to ration her food but Mr Hartigan had saved her the train fare and she was very hungry.

"Hey, young one—give us a crisp."

Candy turned indignantly to stare at the small person who had referred to *her* as a young one. "What age are you?" she asked.

"Ten."

"So am I, so there's no reason for you to call me young one."

"Oh Miss Lah-Di-Dah, high and mighty."

"I am not."

"You sound it."

"I can't help the way I sound."

The other girl seemed to consider this. Then she nodded her head. "Okay. Fair enough."

"Here," Candy produced another packet of crisps. "You can have these."

"Janey, thanks."

For some moments they munched in companionable silence.

"What's your name?"

"Candy."

"I've never heard that name before but I think it's lovely."

"Thanks. What's yours?"

"Sharon."

"I like that too."

They looked at one another shyly. It was hard for Candy to believe that Sharon was ten. She was a good three inches smaller than herself and she was skinny, almost fragile looking. Just looking at her made Candy feel big and somehow clumsy.

"I've run away from home." She offered this as as a token of friendship.

"From home?"

"Well, not from my parents—they're away at the moment. But I couldn't stand the woman who was minding me—she was awful. Nobody will miss me anyway because I have no friends in Howth. What about you? Do you live here—in Kilbarrack I mean?"

"I used to. We moved though and I was just back here having a look around."

Sharon began to tell her story and as Candy listened she felt ashamed of herself and her pampered life.

Sharon's mother had died five years ago when Sharon's little sister was born. Sharon was the middle child with two older and two younger sisters. Her father had managed very well to look after his five daughters with the help of neighbours and their granny who used to come out every weekend to stay with them in Kilbarrack.

Then last Christmas Sharon's father had been made redundant.

He had tried to find more work but two months ago he had given up and gone to England.

"And you didn't go with him?"

"No—how could he go looking for work in London with five kids? Granny said she'd mind us but she wouldn't live in Kilbarrack—she calls it the country. So we all had to move into her flat in Dublin. There's another family living in our house now. They've painted the gate black but I think our blue colour was nicer."

"Do you like living with your Granny?" asked Candy, trying to imagine what it must be like to have your parents gone, one of them forever and the other maybe for years.

"I hate it. Granny's okay but her flat's too small and we all have to sleep in the same bedroom except for Karen and she sleeps with Granny. And Granny gets cranky, she's very old and there's never enough money. I don't know any of the other kids in the flats and I hate my new school. I wish I was back in Kilbarrack. How many brothers and sisters have you got?"

"None."

"You're lucky."

"*I* don't think so, it can be very lonely on your own. I've always wanted a sister at least. I think you're lucky having four."

"That's all you know—they just fight with me and I have to mind the little ones."

"Still."

They finished their crisps in silence and then Sharon grabbed Candy's arm. "Listen, I've had this cool idea. Candy, why don't you and me, the two of us, run away together. We can be sisters then, just the two of us, nobody bossing us or telling us what to do. You've left home, can I come with you?"

"Oh Sharon—would you really? I'd love that more than anything. But—what about your Granny? Wouldn't she come looking for you?"

"Ah, poor Granny. I think she'd be glad if I ran away. I can't help much because I'm not strong and she has an awful lot of work to do. She won't let Imelda help because she says she has to take advantage of her education and Adele is dead lazy—she's in sixth class. If I ran away it would mean less work for Granny and more money for food."

Candy couldn't believe her luck. She

thought of night coming on, of loneliness and cold. It would be great having a companion, a pretend sister. "Right—it's a deal. I have £10 and I'll give you half."

"I couldn't take any money from you," Sharon shook her head, "not unless I was your blood sister. Here, hang on a sec."

She galloped across the road to a grassy island in the middle. Around a lamp-post the grass hadn't been cut and the blades grew tall. It was at these that Sharon was now staring. She walked around deliberating. Then she bent and plucked a blade. She ran this between thumb and finger, then did it again and let out a yelp. Holding the blade of grass aloft, she ran back to Candy. "Look—blood. Now, give us your hand."

Candy held out her hand and closed her eyes. She felt a tickle along the pad of her middle finger and then a sharp but fleeting pain.

"Now." Sharon pressed their two fingers together and held them there with her other hand. "Our bloods have mingled. From this day on we are real blood sisters."

Candy stared at her bloody, grubby finger. "Don't you think we should wash our wounds? You know—in case of germs." She had seen a

documentary film on television the week
before dealing with the dangers of tetanus.

"Oh Miss Lah-Di-Dah—here we go again.
Are you afraid you might get germs from my
common blood?"

Candy felt like giving her now-found sister
a good shake.

"You can be really annoying sometimes,
Sharon—do you know that? It's nothing to do
with your blood being common, it's on account
of germs. Anyone can get them—the Queen of
England could get germs. And anyway, I don't
think you've got common blood, I'm sure it's
every bit as good as mine."

"Ah sorry, Candy. It's just that sometimes I
can't help jeering you, you sound so posh. All
right, come on and we'll get rid of these
germans."

3

Candy Becomes Charlie

"Have you thought about a disguise?"

"What?"

They stood washing their hands at a drinking fountain outside the station. Sharon pointed to Candy's school blazer. "I mean, if Mrs What's-her-Name decided to tell the Gárdaí you'd run away, they wouldn't have a hard time finding you. Have you any other clothes in your schoolbag?"

"Jeans and a jumper."

"Then I think you should get outa that uniform, it's a dead giveaway. Come on, you can change at the Ladies in Connolly station."

"But what will I do with this?" Candy tugged at the lapel of her blazer. "It'd be very bulky to carry around and it wouldn't fit in my schoolbag."

Sharon thought for a minute. Then she said,

20

"We could hock it."

"What?"

"You know—pawn it."

Candy had never been in a pawnshop in her life but she had always believed that they only dealt in things like jewellery. "I don't think a pawn shop would be interested in a school uniform."

"The one near my gran's takes everything."

"We couldn't go there—too dangerous."

Sharon shrugged her shoulders. "Dump it in a bin."

"Talk sense, Sharon. If the Gárdaí found it they'd think I'd been murdered."

They pondered the problem in silence. Then Candy snapped her fingers. "I've got it—give it to a charity shop."

"Come on, let's go," said Sharon, dragging Candy back into the station. "Our adventure is only beginning."

Sitting in DART, staring at the neat back gardens as they whizzed past, Candy thought how lucky she was to have met Sharon. She realized now that if she had been alone she would have been frightened, but with a friend by her side, a blood sister, it was going to be fun. And Sharon *was* fun. Candy believed that they were going to get on well together, better

than she had ever got on with horrible
Siobhán Murtagh.

In the Ladies in Connolly station Candy
folded her school uniform. She stared at her
reflection in the mirror and as she did, an
exciting idea occurred to her. "Sharon, how
about me turning myself into a boy?"

Sharon's mouth dropped open.

"I mean—wouldn't it make sense? It would
be a good disguise and a brother and sister
would be safer than two sisters What do you
say? All I need is a haircut."

Sharon stared at Candy's shining black hair
which fell to her shoulders. "But your hair is
so nice ..." She drew her fingers self-
consciously through her own lack-lustre locks.

"Who cares—it'll grow again."

At first they thought they might buy a
scissors and cut it themselves but they
decided that the last thing they wanted was to
draw attention to themselves. It would be
money well spent to go to a hairdressers.

"Not one of the flash ones around O'Connell
Street," Sharon advised, "they charge you just
to look at you. There are cheaper ones you can
find. Come on, I'll show you."

Candy didn't know Dublin very well but
Sharon seemed familiar with every alley and

lane. She led Candy through a warren of back streets, across bridges, past churches, until she stopped outside an old-fashioned barber's shop. There was a red-and-white pole sticking out of the window. "Now, all you have to do is pretend you're a boy and go in and ask for short back and sides. That's what my Da always got."

Candy stopped in her tracks. "I can't pretend I'm a boy," she said, horrified.

"Then how are you going to pretend to be my brother? Go *on*."

Inside it was surprisingly gloomy. In a big square chair a man sat, draped in white. Another man, also in white, was standing over him, squirting something from a bottle onto the palm of his hand. The air was warm and damp. The man turned to Candy. "Well, love, are you looking for someone?"

"No," squeaked Candy, then tried again, making her voice come low out of her chest. "I want a haircut, short back and sides."

"Well now, I took you for a little girl with all that fancy hair. You kids nowadays, nobody can tell the difference. Anyway, you could certainly do with a haircut. Jerry," he shouted towards the back of the shop. "A young gentleman here for a haircut."

Candy kept her eyes on the floor as she was led to a chair, swathed in a white cape and pushed, none too gently, into a seat.

"Hi!" said Jerry.

Candy mumbled something.

"Why do you want to have all this cut off? It'd look great in a ponytail."

"My parents thought—"

"Yeh—parents can be a real pain. I'm surprise they allowed you to grow it in the first place."

Candy felt a tinge of regret as the scissors began to snip and she saw her black locks fall on the floor. It had taken her three years to grow her hair to this length and it was just right now to put it in a bun for ballet classes.

"This okay?"

Hesitantly she raised her eyes to the mirror. Then stared. She didn't look like Candy O'Brien any more, nobody would recognise her now, she was sure.

"It suits you, I think" said Jerry. "You don't look half bad. A touch of the Michael Jacksons."

Candy smiled at her reflection. She had to admit it: she made quite a handsome boy!

"Janey!" Sharon stared at her as she came out the door. "Your own mother wouldn't know you."

"Do you like it?"

"It looks great."

"Come on then, here, carry my schoolbag."

Sharon folder her arms. "Why should I?"

"Because I'm a boy now and I'm going to boss you around and get you to do things for me."

"That's what *you* think."

"But girls always do things for boys."

"Don't be so soppy, Candy—no boy is going to tell me what to do. Anyway, you're not a boy so stop letting that haircut go to your head."

They both began to laugh at Sharon's unintentional joke.

"You know," Candy said, "I was beginning to think I really was a boy for a while." She picked up her schoolbag and put an arm round Sharon. "Come on—let's get rid of the uniform at the charity shop."

Heading back towards the centre of the city Candy practised walking like a boy. She thought they swaggered around more than girls, throwing their legs out in front of them.

"What are you doing?" asked Sharon, eyeing her with curiosity.

"Walking like a boy."

"You look more like you're practising to be a

kangaroo. Just walk ordinary."

O'Connell Street was full of the smells of frying food—fish, hamburgers, chips.

"I'm starving," they said together, then, "Snap."

"Tell you what. As soon as we get rid of this uniform we'll treat ourselves to our last McDonald's—maybe forever."

Looking up at a clock on a shopfront, Candy was surprised to see that it was already half past three. And all she'd had since breakfast was a packet of crisps. No wonder she was feeling hungry.

It was lovely to sit on a plastic chair in McDonalds and savour every bite of food, chewing thoroughly to make it all last longer. But as the last of her Coke gurgled up through her straw, Candy began to think of the night ahead. Suddenly she didn't feel brave any more and running away from home didn't seem such a good idea. Where would they sleep? She looked at Sharon but Sharon was slowly licking each finger, an expression of bliss on her face. "That was great, Candy— thanks. My Da hardly ever brought us to McDonalds—there were just too many of us."

"Sharon—where will we sleep tonight?"

"Dunno. Haven't thought."

"Well, think now."

Eventually they decided to go back to the DART and travel on it out to Dun Laoire where Sharon said they could sleep in one of the shelters on the pier.

"How much money have we left?" she asked.

Candy began to count. "Five pounds and seventy p."

"We can't spend any more money on train fares then."

"Then how are we going to get to Dun Laoire? Walk?"

"No, I've got a plan."

Half an hour later passengers entering the Connolly Street DART station were greeted by the pathetic sight of a little girl crying inconsolably while her big brother wiped away her tears.

Most people passed by, some throwing them sympathetic looks. Eventually a lady with grey hair approached them. "What's wrong dear? Why are you crying?"

Sharon's sobs reached a crescendo but Candy answered in her most polite voice. "My sister is upset, Madam, because she lost our trainfare home. We've no money at all so we can't even phone our parents. It will only take us a few hours to walk home. I've been trying to convince her that we can easily walk."

"Good gracious me," said the woman. "Of course you cannot walk. Here, what do you need? Is £2 enough? Now little girl, dry your tears and hurry home. Your parents will be getting worried."

It seemed like old times being back on the DART and it seemed like a million years since Candy had set out by herself that morning. The train felt more luxurious than before, its seats softer, its air warm. Candy wondered suddenly would it be cold at night, even in May.

4

Mrs Allen

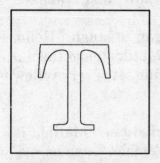

he friends stretched their legs but had to gather them in quickly as the train began to fill up. As they left the station people were standing, and Candy said, pointing to an elderly lady dressed in purple, "I'd better offer her a seat, she's got a baby."

When Candy approached the woman however, she got a fright. The baby's pink-bonnetted head turned towards her and Candy found herself staring at the hairy face of a monkey.

"Thank you, young man," the woman said in a haughty tone and heaved herself in beside Sharon. Along with the monkey she was carrying several shopping bags, and Sharon helped her to stow them in at her feet.

"Such nice children," the woman said. "I always think that children are a great improvement on their parents and so does Matilda. Say hello to the little girl, Matilda."

The monkey set up a fearful chatter. Then she shot out a scaly paw and tweaked Sharon's ear.

Sharon and Candy began to laugh. "Hello, Matilda," they said and Matilda gave them a wide smile, displaying a fine set of very yellow teeth.

"It's cute," said Candy.

Matilda's owner corrected her. "Matilda is not an it, she is a she. Female, same as me. She's my baby and a very good baby too. Of course," she began to whisper in Sharon's ear, "she's not really a baby—she's quite elderly in fact, just like me! But she doesn't know, so we don't tell her. She thinks she's a baby, that's why I dress her like one."

Matilda and her owner chattered away until the train was approaching Blackrock when the woman began to look around her in a worried sort of way. "This is the worse part. I hate getting off trains and buses. So much bother, and I always forget something."

"We'll help," Sharon suggested. "We can get off here and help you with your packages, can't we—Charlie?"

She had to dig Candy in the ribs as she

failed to recognised her new name.

"Of course we can."

Candy bent to pick up a bag.

It was a strange little procession that left Blackrock station, with the woman's long purple garments whirling in the breeze, the monkey making a loud whooping noise and the children staggering under the weight of a variety of shopping bags. Candy wondered what on earth they contained.

"I live just around the corner. You must come in and have some tea after your kind deed." The woman beamed down at them. "By the way, my name is Mrs Allen but you may call me Minerva."

"And I'm Sharon," Sharon swallowed, "Minerva. And this is my brother, Charlie."

Her house was small and neat with shining door brasses and sparkling windows. "Now, dump those bags and come into the sitting room. I want you to meet the rest of the family."

As she opened the sitting room door, a gruff voice said, "And about time too."

The friends stared at one another but Mrs Allen only laughed. "Don't pay any attention to Mabel—she's cross because I took Matilda instead of her. Now children, come and be introduced. This is Mabel."

"How d'you do," said a large green parrot and winked at them.

"And this is Minnie." The little white mouse went whirling madly round its wheel.

"This is Mona but she's feeling poorly. She watched too much T.V. last night and it really doesn't agree with her." The goldfish did look exhausted, barely moving in its glass bowl.

"And that's the whole family and I can see that they've taken a shine to you already."

Mrs Allen sat down and motioned the children to a sofa opposite. "Now, tea. We must have some tea and lots of cake. I *love* cakes. Maggie," she shouted.

"Maggie," echoed the parrot, and Matilda began to clap her hands and laugh hysterically.

Then the door opened and a woman, older than Mrs Allen, entered. She was dressed in a black skirt and white apron and on her head she wore a mob cap, the type that used to be worn by servants in bygone days.

"Maggie, we have visitors for tea so I want you to make one of your specials. This is Sharon and her brother Charlie."

"Pleased to meet you," said Maggie.

"Likewise," said Mabel.

When the tea arrived it was pushed in on a trolley by Maggie. The two girls stared in disbelief. There was chocolate cake, apple tart, fairy buns with cherries on the top. There were meringues sandwiched with cream, eclairs covered in chocolate sauce, a sponge cake covered in pink sugar and a tipsy cake.

"Now children, I hope you will do justice to Maggie's tea. She's baked every single item herself and she will be insulted if you don't try everything."

The girls did not have to be asked twice. However, hungry as they were, they could not compete with Mrs Allen. Matilda also had a healthy appetite and Mabel had some tea, half of which she spewed out of her beak.

Mrs Allen raised the last morsel of meringue to her lips and poured another cup of tea. "I really don't know why I'm so inclined to put on weight," she sighed. "I mean, I eat very little, really. I don't eat cabbage or parsnips or lettuce. I seldom eat chops and never eat stew and still the pounds go on." She patted an ample hip which shook like a jelly. "Life is so unfair, isn't it?"

The girls nodded in solemn agreement but Mabel wasn't so polite. "Chocolate," she cackled. "Chocolate will be the ruination of

Minerva."

Mrs Allen turned to Candy. "I wonder if you'd mind, little boy—Charlie—would you give Maggie a hand in the kitchen? I just want to have a word with your sister."

When Candy had wheeled out the trolley Mrs Allen took Sharon's hand. "I was wondering, dear—would you like to stay her with me for a while—be my guest?"

Sharon stared at her. "But what about Can—Charlie?"

"That's the other thing I wanted to talk to you about. Of course he'd stay here, he'd have to if you were. But I couldn't have him around me. I cannot abide the male sex in any shape or form."

Sharon was about to explain that Charlie was really Candy when Mrs Allen added, "Boys and lies, I cannot abide either."

Sharon began to think. It was fun here with Mrs Allen and all the animals. And the grub was terrific. "I'd have to ask Charlie. And where would he live if you didn't want him around you?"

"He could stay with Maggie. Of course I wouldn't expect him to do any work, just keep to the kitchen. And I'd let him have the use of the front garden and he could come in here and visit the family when I was out. You see, it's nothing personal, I'm sure he's a perfectly nice boy—as boys go. Now, off you go and see what he says."

Candy was furious. "I'm not going to skulk in the kitchen while you have all the fun with Minerva. Maggie doesn't even talk to me. I wouldn't even mind if I *were* a boy. It's just not fair."

"Ah come on," Sharon put an arm round her. "Just for a few days. Think of all the food, and the fun we can have with Matilda and Mabel when Mrs Allen's out. What do you say? Just for a couple of days."

They stayed for three days and in the end it was Sharon who wanted to leave. Candy found life in the kitchen very peaceful and she quite enjoyed helping Maggie to bake. However, she did get fed up eating the result of Maggie's baking, for there was little else in the house to eat except cakes. Candy would not have believed that she would have ever thought with longing of Mrs Nolan's watery stews, but when yet another slice of chocolate cake was presented to her at dinner time, she would have given anything for a carrot or potato or even a bit of gristly meat.

It was not the food that worried Sharon so

Candy on the DART

much as the lack of sleep. She had grown quite fond of Mrs Allen, for in spite of her many eccentricities she turned out to be a very kind woman and a lonely one. Maybe this was why she talked so much, why she followed Sharon around, telling her stories about her pets, living and dead.

Sharon never managed to get to bed before eleven, but even then she had little chance of a night's sleep. Hardly had she closed her eyes than there would be a knock on her door and Mrs Allen, her long grey hair tied back with a pink ribbon, would come in and sit down on the bed. "Here, I've brought us a snack." More tea and cake. "Now I must tell you about Isabella. She was my first monkey and I had great difficulty getting her into the country ..."

Sharon often dozed off but Mrs Allen would shake her awake.

At the end of three days Sharon could stand it no longer. "We've got to get out of here," she told Candy. "I'll die of lack of sleep if we don't."

"Or we'll both die of cake poisoning. But what will we say?"

They decided to tell her the truth, which turned our to be a good idea, for Mrs Allen was enchanted at the idea of running away from home.

"What an adventure!" she said, clapping her hands, and Matilda clapped hers too. "I wish I didn't have so many family responsibilities or I'd come with you. Of course I see that you cannot stay here with me. You must be out on the highways and byways. You must have a proper adventure."

"You know," said Candy as they made their way once more to the DART station, "I don't think staying with Mrs Allen was such a good idea. I think it softened us up. I mean, I feel quite scared all over again and we have the problem of where we are going to sleep tonight."

"Dun Laoire of course," Sharon replied. "Remember that's what we originally planned. Come on, cheer up. The sun is shining."

5

A Night in the Open

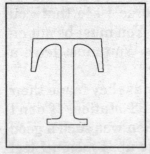

The sea in Dun Laoire harbour was calm and blue. There was no wind and all the little yachts lay idle in the sunshine. The mailboat was berthed, waiting to make its nightly journey to Holyhead.

"We could become stowaways," said Sharon, pointing towards the boat. "I mean, if we ever get fed up with life in Ireland."

The pier was full of bustle—men fishing, children and dogs running back and forth, older people walking at a more leisurely pace. Forgetting about the night to come, the two girls headed for the rocks. "Let's play pirates."

"No. Explorers."

"Okay—half and half. Pirates first and then explorers."

So absorbed did they become in their game that they didn't notice the shadows lengthening and the activity on the pier grow less and less. Suddenly their game was brought to a halt by a shout from the pier. "Hey."

They turned to see a tall man dressed in a black coat standing a couple of yards away.

"What are you children doing down here by yourselves? It's getting dark. Shouldn't you be heading home?"

Candy could hear her teeth begin to chatter but Sharon merely tossed her head. "Who said we were on our own, Mister? Our Da's with us. He's gone down them slippery rocks to get his fishing tackle. He told us to wait here in case we slipped."

The man continued to stare at them.

"He's coming back now with Jaws. He's our Alsation, Mister, and our Da has to keep a hold of him because he bites strangers. Here he comes now. Come on Jaws, good boy."

Sharon let out a shrill whistle and the man, turning on his heel, walked back up the pier.

Candy looked at her friend admiringly. "Gosh! You're very brave. And clever. I'd never have thought of saying all that."

Sharon smiled. "It was nothing. Come on, it's nearly dark and we'd better find a sleeping place."

Although they had planned to sleep in one of the shelters, neither girl now wanted to go back onto the pier. There might be all sorts of people up there, and it seemed very high and exposed to the wind which had begun to rise.

"We could sleep in the cave," Candy suggested. This was not really a cave, more a hollow between two rocks which they had found earlier when they had been playing pirates. "At least we'd be protected from the wind."

Carefully they made their way across the rocks, for it was now becoming difficult to see. When they found the place they burrowed into it like little animals, wrapping their arms around one another for warmth and comfort. The noise of the waves breaking seemed very loud and Candy wondered how she had not noticed it at all earlier in the evening.

"I'll never get to sleep this night," said Sharon. "These rocks are too hard."

Candy believed that terror would keep her awake until dawn. The wind moaned around their little hollow and the beam of a lighthouse out in the bay cut across the darkness, turning the rocks a ghostly silver. Candy thought of her bedroom in Howth and Mrs Nolan in the kitchen drinking gin. Just across the bay lay home, and even if Mrs Nolan was a terror, she was human, not a ghost. Candy snuggled closer to Sharon. "If I live till dawn," she promised herself, "I'll go home tomorrow and never, ever run away again."

Eventually, through sheer exhaustion, both girls fell asleep. It was the sun that woke them next morning, shining on their faces, warming their stiff limbs. Sharon stood up. "Come on, I'll race you to the end of the pier."

They felt better after their run, as blood began to course through arms and legs. The sun sparkled on the water; the sky above was without a cloud. As far as they could tell, they were the only two people awake in the whole world.

Sharon looked at Candy. "How about a dip?"

"But we've no togs."

"We don't need them—there's nobody to see us."

The water was shockingly cold, forcing them to move with vigour. Candy did a graceful crawl and although Sharon looked odd, twisting her head from side to side, she moved through the water with speed.

Afterwards they ran up and down the pier, shaking the water from their naked bodies.

Their clothes felt wonderful when they put them back on, so soft and warm. They lay down on their backs and closed their eyes against the sun.

"I don't care how little money we have," Candy said, "I'll have to have something to eat before I die of hunger."

Sharon shook her head lazily. "You might as well have a snooze, no shops will be open yet. I'd say it's only about seven o'clock."

They didn't really sleep again but they dozed. This morning, Candy had changed her mind about running away and once more it seemed like a brilliant idea. There was no school looming, no homework, no adults around to tell them what they could or couldn't do.

When they got to Dun Laoire it was still very early but they found a corner shop open where they bought some rolls and two small cartons of milk. They sauntered back to the pier and sat once more in the sunshine to have their breakfast.

Licking her fingers, Sharon said, "I'm not spending another night out here, Candy. I was really scared last night."

Candy, who had imagined that nothing would scare her friend, was pleased by this admission.

"I'll tell you what," she suggested, "why don't we spend the morning here and then we can head into town for the afternoon? When we're in town we can think about what we want to do."

When they had finished eating and had placed the rubbish in a bin, they walked down onto the rocks, well away from the pier and from the attention of any nosey parkers who might wonder why two young girls were not at school.

"Candy."

"H'mm?"

"I saw a ghost last night." Sharon was staring straight ahead of her, out into the bay.

Candy lifted her chin. "I don't believe you. I don't believe in ghosts anyway."

"Why were you so scared then last night and holding onto me?"

"I wasn't—I was just cold."

"I saw a big, black shape coming up from the sea and a sort of flopping sound. I—"

"Stop it. I don't want to hear any more."

Even in broad daylight, Candy was scared, which was why she didn't want Sharon talking about it. "Just shut up, Sharon, I'm going to lie back and try to get to sleep. When

I wake up you might be able to talk some sense."

She lay back and closed her eyes. She must have dozed off but suddenly she was awake again, listening to some noise above the breaking of the waves. What was it? A sort of flip-flop, flip-flop. And it was coming nearer. Candy screwed her eyes tight, too terrified to look. She stretched out a hand and grabbed Sharon's, which had been moving tremblingly towards hers.

"I told you," Sharon's voice was a wail. "It's exactly the same sound as last night."

Then Candy screamed as something wet brushed her cheek and she felt a horrible hot breath all over her. She opened her eyes, and standing there, looking down at her with some curiosity, was a large, black labrador.

The two girls sat up and stared at him. He yawned hugely, wagged his tail and lay down beside them.

"There's your ghost," said Candy, laughing. "I'd say this is where he lives. He's obviously a stray."

He looked rather neglected and had no collar.

"Here," said Sharon, offering him the last of her roll which she had been saving for later.

"You probably need this more than I do."

It was fun playing with Blackie in the sunshine. They threw sticks into the water for him and admired how he swam after them. They ran along the pier with him, screeching as he showered them with sea water. They scolded him when he barked at the seagulls and they hid him when they saw other dogs approach, their owners just a few steps behind.

It was only when they bent to pat him goodbye that they realized they had a problem.

"Just walk away," Sharon suggested, "he won't follow for long."

But he did. When *they* ran, *he* ran; when they walked he trotted along beside them, tail in the air.

"Go home," said Sharon. "Shoo." She stamped her foot at him. For a moment he stopped and then he began to creep after them again, his tail now between his legs.

"Poor Blackie," said Sharon. "Look how sad he is."

"Don't be thick, Candy. We can't run away with a dog along with us. And we haven't even enough money to buy food for ourselves."

"Well, we can't just abandon him. And it's

your fault anyway. You encouraged him in the first place with that bit of roll."

During this exchange, Blackie stood in front of them, a hopeful expression in his brown eyes.

"I suppose you're right," Sharon finally agreed, "but don't encourage him. Sort of ignore him until we get to the DART station and he may get fed up with us and just go off by himself."

6

Blackie Stays

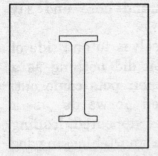n the back of the Mercedes, Candy stretched her legs. Sharon had done it again. When the man at the station had said, "No dogs on the DART," Candy had been resigned to either walking into Dublin or spending another night on Dun Laoire pier. She knew that Blackie could not now be abandoned; for better or worse he was now their dog.

She had reckoned without Sharon however. A familiar expression had come into Sharon's eyes and she had said, "I've got a plan. Come on."

She led them through the streets of the town, up to a house where a brass plate proclaimed, V.E. Browne, Veterinary Surgeon, and an arrow below pointed to the surgery.

Candy looked at her friend in horror. "Sharon—you're not going to have Blackie put down?"

"Don't be thick. Anyway, where would we get the money? Just stand here and say nothing."

They positioned themselves to one side of the surgery door. Sharon did nothing as a variety of owners and their pets came out. Eventually she stepped forwards as a glamorous looking woman appeared, leading a golden labrador, a much smarter looking dog than poor Blackie.

"Excuse me," said Sharon in a refined voice. "I wonder could we speak to you, please?"

The tale she told had Candy almost in tears. Blackie had belonged to a very old woman who, when she died, left him to her son to look after. The son, however, had simply thrown the poor dog on the street and now the children in the street tormented him and threw stones at him. One had even burned him with a cigarette. So Sharon and her brother—Candy looked up in momentary surprise—because they were too poor to offer him a home themselves, were taking him to the Cats and Dogs Home in Dublin. As they weren't allowed to take him on the DART, would the lady be kind enough to give them a lift, even a little bit of the way?

"What kind little children you are!" the lady had cried. "Of course I'll take you into town. Just wait until I get Bella in first—she'd better sit in the front with me or she'd be jealous. What's your dog called?" She addressed the question to Candy.

Sharon had pushed herself forward. "Don't ask him—he's deaf and dumb but he knows sign language. Hey, Charlie."

Candy got a dig in the ribs and tried to keep a straight face as she watched Sharon making funny signs with her fingers. She replied by touching her head and her nose and rubbing her forehead.

"He says thanks very much and to tell you that Blackie is a very well behaved dog."

"I'm sure he is," said the woman, looking mesmerized.

Now Candy smiled again, remembering the woman's expression. Beside her, Sharon was leaning forward, chatting away, and at their feet Blackie had fallen asleep, overcome by all the luxury.

"It was very hard for Ma," Sharon was saying, "when Da was lost at sea. It turned her mind a bit. She still goes down to the harbour every night, thinking she'll see his boat coming in, even though there was a funeral and everything. So Charlie and I have to look after the little ones. There's not much money but we manage."

When they arrived at the Cats and Dogs Home the woman let them out of the back of the car and pressed a £5 note into Sharon's hand. "Here you are, my dear, this is for your fares home. You are not only kind children but you are immensely brave too."

As the car disappeared round the corner Sharon did a handstand. "Yippee! What do you think of that—five quid?"

"That's all very well," said Candy sulkily, "but why did I have to be deaf and dumb?"

"You talk too posh. She'd never have believed we were poor if she heard you talk. Then we'd have got no money. Isn't this the life, Candy? No school, swims before breakfast and drives in Mercedes."

"You're an awful liar, Sharon, do you know that?"

Sharon tossed her head. "Them's not lies, Candy O'Brien. Them's inventions."

The girls began to walk towards the city centre, Blackie bounding along beside them. He seemed delighted with his new owners, and for their part, even though they had found him only that morning, they could not now imagine themselves without him. They soon discovered, however, that the life of a dog owner was not all sunshine. Blackie, who had become quite cocky by now, seemed to think that he owned the pavements and got very annoyed with other dogs who wanted to walk there also. There were many places where dogs weren't allowed and others where they had to be on a lead. The girls decided that they would have to buy one. "But we'll get him something to eat first," Candy suggested. "There wasn't much nourishment in that bit of roll."

At a butcher's shop they bought some scraps and the butcher gave them a large juicy bone for nothing. Then they bought chips and Mars bars for themselves and decided to have a picnic in Stephen's Green.

It seemed a beautiful park to Candy. The flower beds were full of colour; fat, happy ducks swam in the lake and the water of the fountains sparkled in the sunshine.

"We often come her on a Sunday, since we moved in with Granny," Sharon said, leading the way to a special picnic spot that she knew. "There's a children's playground over there but it's only for little kids."

It was warm in the Green, more so than it had been in Dun Laoire. Blackie lay under a bush with his tongue out, with hardly enough energy to growl if someone approached his bone. The girls lay on the grass and kicked their heels.

"Do you know what," said Sharon, not looking up from the daisy chain she was making.

"M'mm?" Candy was too lazy to open her mouth.

"I think it's great having you for a blood sister. I think we should take a vow to remain sisters, whatever happens."

Solemnly they stood up, clasped hands, and with their eyes turned up towards the sky, vowed to remain blood sisters for life. Candy felt a bit silly standing there, but still, she was pleased by what Sharon had said.

The awkward moment was broken by Blackie who had stood up also and now began to howl, staring like them up into the sky.

Both girls began to laugh and Candy stooped to pat Blackie's head. "Okay, you can be our blood brother. That's what you want—isn't it?"

7

The Derelict House

"What are we going to do?" Candy moaned.

It was five o'clock in the afternoon and the sky was as dark as night. Rain fell in sheets and Candy and Sharon stared at it from the shelter of a shop doorway. Blackie lay at their feet, his nose resting on his feet, looking depressed.

Sharon sneezed. "I hope I'm not getting a cold."

"You might get pneumonia and I'd have to have you rushed into hospital."

"That's right, cheer me up."

"At least you'd have a bed for the night."

The two friends were fast discovering that a wet night was no fun when you had no home to go to. And tonight would be colder than last night too. Candy wondered why she had been foolish enough to give away her school uniform as she shivered inside her thin sweater.

Suddenly Sharon nudged her. "I've got it. I know where we can sleep tonight."

"Where?"

"It's a house about two streets away from Gran's. There was a fire there and part of it was burned down. Most of it's okay though and I know a way in at the back. I used to go exploring round there and I found it one day."

They brought three packets of crisps to celebrate and ate them in the doorway while they waited for the rain to stop. After about ten minutes it had thinned to a drizzle and they set off, across the Halfpenny Bridge and up through Temple Bar.

As they walked on, the streets became shabbier, with more derelict buildings around. Soon, however, these gave way to narrower streets with rows of small, neat houses.

"Gran lives over there," said Sharon pointing, "but we turn left now."

Candy did not like the look of the house when they came to it. The windows and doors were boarded up. The grass in the tiny front garden was inches high. "Sharon," she said, "suppose there are rats?" One of Candy's great fears was rats.

"Rats," Sharon scoffed. "What about Blackie? No rat would come near us once he got a smell of Blackie."

They made their way round to the back of the house where Sharon pointed to a small window. "Those boards are loose, or at least they were." She began to shove at them with her elbow and they soon gave in. "Now—have we got everything—food, torch, Blackie's bone? We're going to be quite cosy here tonight."

They found themselves in what seemed like some sort of kitchen. There was a sink and a gas cooker and even some dilapidated chairs. Candy felt her spirits rise. "This doesn't look too bad at all."

"And we can tidy it in the morning. We can take down the boards so's we can see and give it a real springclean. This is our new home. How about that, Candy?"

They ate their sandwiches and apples and gave Blackie a dog biscuit and his bone. Then they lay back on the chairs, and although they hadn't intended to, they were so tired that they both fell asleep.

It was Blackie's barking that awoke them. Candy felt Sharon stir and stretch a hand towards her. "Sh'sh—there's someone there."

As they sat listening, the kitchen door was stealthily opened and the beam from a torch began to play over their faces.

"What have we got here then?" a gruff voice asked. "Get the lamp, George, till we see what we've got here."

The torch beam was withdrawn and in the darkness they listened to a match being struck. The kitchen filled with a dim, yellowish light.

Candy saw a large man with a black beard and wild looking black hair. Behind him, holding the lamp, was a small, skinny youth who looked about sixteen.

The tall man stretched out both arms and grabbed the two girls. Blackie ran at him, snapping at his heels but with a vicious kick the man sent him sprawling into a corner.

"You leave our dog alone," said Candy, her anger overcoming her fear.

The man drew them closer in his grasp, glaring into their faces. "You've got a cheek, breaking into my house and then telling me what to do."

"It's not your house," Sharon answered him. "You've no more right here than we have. I knew the family that used to live here before it was burned down and you're not one of them."

George came forward. "Can I get rid of them for you, boss? I can do it easy—it'd be a pleasure."

Candy, no longer brave, began to shiver with fear.

But the big man's attitude to them seemed to have changed. He was smiling at them, a horrible leer exposing blackened teeth. "Well, my dears, sit down and let us get to know one another. And tell me—what brought you to this house? Come on now, sit, make yourselves comfortable."

Somehow his friendliness was more frightening than his previous roughness; both girls knew that he was just pretending, but they didn't know why.

Hesitantly they began to tell him their story. Sharon, so good at making up tales, was now too frightened to tell him anything but the truth; Candy blurted out straight away that she was really a girl.

When they had finished speaking, the two men walked away, taking the lamp with them. In the darkness Candy listened to their whispering. Maybe they were discussing a method of killing them. She put one hand over her mouth and with the other grabbed Sharon. At their feet Blackie began to whimper. Sharon bent towards him. "Please stop, Blackie. Stop it or they'll hurt you again."

The men returned, smiling. "Well now, young ladies, George and I have decided that you can stay here. We wouldn't turn two homeless kids onto the street, would we, George?"

"No way, Boss."

"And to show how kind we are, we're even going to allow you to keep that dog. However—I expect something in return. You've got to earn your keep. Does that seem fair to you?"

They nodded, wondering fearfully what he had in store.

"It'll just be a question of helping us out now and again. Doing a few messages for us. What do you say to that?"

Again they both nodded.

"George and I run a little business from this house—we've borrowed it, in a sense, until we get out new premises. You two will be our junior partners." He laughed horribly. "Now, George, we might as well introduce our new partners to our line of business. Set things up, like a good lad."

The girls watched in fascination as George

began to take up floorboards. Then he reached down and took up what looked like a steel suitcase. He placed it in front of the man, who began to fiddle around with a lock on the front of it. "This is a combination lock but only the senior partner knows the combination. Right, George?"

With a click, the lid of the suitcase sprang upwards. From it the man withdrew first a delicate looking weighing scales and then a large package wrapped in black plastic.

When the black plastic was removed, the girls saw that the package contained a white substance, finer than salt. With a measuring spoon, George began to weigh this substance carefully, pausing to read the scales as he put a spoonful on it. When he got the quantity he wanted he tipped it into a small plastic bag which he then sealed.

When he had filled ten bags, he handed them to the man and began to replace everything in the suitcase. Once all the floorboards were back in place, he stood up. "Ready when you are, Boss."

"Now, my dears, just follow me. And don't think about running away or causing any trouble. You might just get hurt." As he said this he gave each girl's arm a painful pinch.

"We're just going to take you for a little drive."

George got into the front of the car and the man sat behind with a girl on either side. On his lap was a black leather briefcase which contained the ten packages.

They drove for about ten minutes and then the man said, "Now this is your introduction to your new career, so watch carefully how it's done."

They sat in the car for a second while George stared all around him. Then he said, "All clear," and the man got out, beckoning the girls after him. They walked to the end of a quiet street and up to the door of a shabby looking house. The man rang the bell and it was answered immediately by a skinny young woman with red eyes. She didn't say anything, just stretched out a hand for the package.

"These are your contacts from now on," the man told her, pointing to Sharon and Candy. "Either one or other or them will make the delivery. Look at them and remember their faces. They'll be dressed in either blue or yellow to make it easier for you."

There were nine more stops and at each one the procedure was the same. Sometimes a man opened the door, sometimes a woman. All of them looked unhappy and unwell.

As they were driving back to the derelict house, the man gave his horrible smile. "You work for me and you even get a uniform—blue and yellow, dead smart."

8

Captured

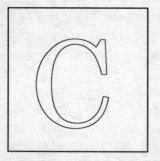

andy listened to Sharon whimpering in her sleep. They didn't have a regular sleep pattern any more, no bed time as such. They simply slept in snatches when exhaustion overcame their fear. Since the batteries of their torch had run out, they were permanently in the dark and had no idea whether it was night or day. They had lost count of time, too, and didn't know how long they had been locked up in the house. From time to time, George brought them food, quite nice food—hamburgers and chips and Coke to drink. Neither girl had any appetite however, and Blackie ate most of what they were given. George also brought Blackie out for walks and the girls were glad that it was George who did this and not the man.

At first they had been very brave. When

they had been locked in the first night and had tried but failed to find a means of escape, Sharon had said, "Our only hope is to make a break for it when we're delivering the drugs."

"Drugs?" The very word made Candy shiver.

"Of course—that's the only reason we're still alive—he thought we'd be useful to him making the deliveries."

"I hope we get caught, by the Gárdaí I mean."

"So do I. And I hope it's the first time."

Since that night however, they had not seen the man and had not been asked to make any deliveries. The two girls had begun to lose hope. It was so frightening to be constantly in the dark, and in the long, idle hours it was hard not to give in to despair and believe that they would never escape. Candy couldn't allow herself to think about her parents or she would begin to cry. It now seemed to her that she had been very foolish to run away. She could blame nobody for the predicament she was in, only herself.

Sharon stirred and sat up, as sounds from the corridor reached the kitchen. Bolts were pulled back and the room filled with the now familiar light from the hurricane lamps. The man stood there, with George peering over his shoulder.

"Good evening, my dears," the man said. "You are going to work this evening. Now, here's your uniforms. You can change in here while George and I do our measuring outside."

The girls watched while George took up the floorboards and lifted out the steel suitcase. When they were alone once more and the door was closed, Sharon turned to Candy. "Now's our chance. We'll have to make a break for it when they let us out. I don't care if they kill us. I'd rather die out there than die a prisoner in this room."

Candy swallowed. She agreed with everything Sharon said but she didn't know if she'd be brave enough to carry the plan through. She imagined a knife in her back or the man's horrible hands around her neck.

There was a polite knock on the door. "Ready, young ladies?" The man's face appeared and his smile seemed even more sinister than usual. "Now George—which one will it be? Which is more suitable for the first run? This one," he pointed to Candy, "is tall. But no—I think the other might be tougher."

The girls stared at one another despairingly.

"But aren't we—" Candy couldn't finish the

sentence as she saw their last hope vanish.

Sharon walked up to the man, brave as a little terrier. "We're going together, remember, Mister. That's what you said the first day, that we'd do the messages together."

The man sniggered. "These girls must think we are very stupid, right George? Think I'd let you both out together, think I'm that much of a fool? *You* go and *you* stay here as a hostage." He grabbed Candy roughly by the shoulder then turned round to face Sharon. "And if you don't do exactly as you're told you'll never see your friend alive again."

Both girls were now trembling.

"Remember," he went on. "Do anything silly and George tells me and I slit your friend's throat. And don't think you'd escape either. We'd get you, wherever you'd run to. Now," with a sudden change of personality he was smiling again. "All you have to do is behave yourselves and everything will be fine. There may even be a bonus for you if everything goes well. How do you girls like ice-cream?"

Candy was very brave. She kissed Sharon good-bye and told her not to worry, even though her knees were knocking together. When the door closed she realized that what she was most afraid of was being left alone with the man. She was afraid of him in a way that she was not afraid of George. He was evil, she could imagine that he would actually enjoy hurting people.

He turned to her and pointed to a chair. "Sit down over there, girl, and don't disturb me, I've got work to do. And don't start snivelling or I won't be able to concentrate."

Candy sat where she was told and Blackie crept up and put his head on her lap. They sat like this, silent and tense, listening to the rustles which the man made as he turned over pages.

She must have fallen asleep for the next thing she knew was George's voice saying, "Went like a dream, Boss, we've got a great little operator here. And I took the liberty of getting some ice-cream. I think it's well deserved."

The man rubbed his hands together and beamed round the kitchen. "Isn't this cosy? We're just like one, big happy family here. Now, George, dish up the ice-cream and we'll leave these young ladies to have an early night. And congratulations, my dear," he patted Sharon on the head. "I knew we could depend on you."

9

At Least We Have Light

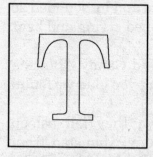hat night was the very worst that the two friends had spent together. Up till now, they had had some hope of escaping but tonight that hope had died.

"The worst thing was," said Sharon as they huddled together in the dark, "that I was really scared in case a policeman came along. All I could think about was what would happen to you and Blackie if I didn't get back."

"Yes," sighed Candy, "he's very clever, he's thought of everything. I don't see how we can ever escape now. What's it like outside?"

"Sunny—it's beautiful. I never realized how beautiful the world was before." Sharon began to cry. "Trees and grass and clouds and sky. And my Da. I want my Da."

"And I want mine," Candy wailed. "And my mother. Oh why did we ever decide to run away—why were we so mad?"

Blackie, who had been lapping up what was left of the ice-cream, came over now to see what was troubling his young friends. Soon his howls had joined theirs and he sounded so pitiful that both girls stopped crying and bent to comfort him.

"Whatever happens," said Candy, "Blackie is going where we go. Aren't you glad we found him that day, Sharon?"

Once they settled down they fell asleep quite quickly for they were exhausted from nerves and tears. When Candy woke up she could tell from the tenseness of Sharon's body beside her that she was already awake. "Are you okay?" she asked.

"Yes … I've been thinking. Candy."

"What?"

"He can't go on just treating us like this. We're useful to him now and we can make demands. I didn't think of it before because all we thought about was escaping. If we have to live here for—for a while, at least we must have light. Otherwise we're going to go nuts."

Candy had to agree. There was no point in pretending that they we going to escape at any minute, they had to be realistic and try to improve their life in this room. Otherwise she feared that Sharon was right—they would go bonkers.

Next day when George came with their food they were ready with their demands.

"We want to see the man," Sharon demanded.

"You mean the boss?" George seemed surprised, even scared.

"Yes and we want to see him today. Just you go and tell him what we said. Now. It's important."

Once they were alone Sharon said, "We'd better eat this food, we'll need all our strength for this interview. Sorry Blackie, you'll have to do with dog food today."

They didn't have long to wait. They knew from the loudness of the approach that the man was in a temper. They stood up together and grasped one another's hands.

"Well?" The man stood there, his black eyes glittering evilly. "What's this I hear then? Think you can start making demands, do you?"

"Yes," they both answered.

"Go on." There was a threat in those two words but Sharon spoke up bravely. "Mister, we know we can't escape, we have to live here, but now that we're working for you we want better conditions."

"We want light for a start."

"And soap and toothpaste."

"But the light's the most important. We *must* have light."

"Hey!"

To their surprise the man didn't seem to be angry any longer. He was smiling and nudging George in the ribs. "I like a bit of spirit in a kid—I always have. You girls stick with me and George and you'll be okay. Now, let's all sit down and see what we can work out."

"I thought they would never go," said Sharon half an hour later.

"Yes, but at least we've got something," replied Candy, sighing with the pleasure of sitting in the lamp light.

The man had left them the hurricane lamp and had promised that tomorrow George would rig up some sort of electricity. They in turn had to promise not to go near the boarded up windows. "If you do, you'll not be rescued— you'll just be dead. Remember that." The menace had returned to the man's voice. "If I see that you are behaving yourselves, and provided that you are good little messengers, then you'll end up quite comfortably, that I promise."

Sharon began to walk around the room now. "It's great to be able to move around again— isn't it? Look, Blackie thinks so too. He wants to play."

Candy didn't join in the fun, however, for she was thinking about her parents. Had they returned from the Himalayas yet? Were they at this moment searching for her, somewhere in Ireland. She wished she knew how long Sharon and she had been locked up for and what date it was. She wondered if they would ever be found. Maybe the man would die—be run over by a bus or killed by another drug baron. If that happened they might never escape, they might starve to death, getting weaker and weaker in this room.

"What's up, Candy?" Sharon, turning round, caught the expression of terror on her friend's face.

"Nothing, I'm okay really." Candy tried to shake the frightening thoughts from her head. "Come on, I want to play. Let's see if we can get Blackie to jump over the table."

And Candy got up to join her two friends.

10

Candy Gets Caught

he kitchen had been transformed. It looked like a miniature house now with a section for sleeping in, Blackie's quarters and a living area.

The girls had no idea how long they had been living as prisoners. Sharon had made two more deliveries of drugs and the man, being pleased with her, had given them things—sleeping bags and a brush for sweeping the floor. He had also given Sharon a watch after her last delivery.

Last night the man had arrived and said to Candy, "Tomorrow, my dear, is your big day. Tomorrow *you* are going to work. We have to have you earning your keep, and as George and I have been thinking of expanding our business we could do with two messengers doing different runs for us. So tomorrow you start. Be ready at eleven o'clock."

It was almost eleven now and the girls sat and listened. Suddenly they heard the now familiar sounds of bolts being withdrawn. "Don't worry now," Sharon whispered. "Just relax and do what George tells you. He could take you to the country or a park or anywhere. It's somewhere different each time."

The man walked in, followed by George. He nodded approvingly when he saw that Candy was dressed in her 'uniform'. "Good girl. Now just sit over there until George is ready for you. And remember everything I've told you— you don't want to be responsible for anything nasty happening to your friend."

Candy's legs felt as if they would collapse under her as she made her way to George's car. The daylight hurt her eyes although today the sky was quite overcast.

She sat in beside George and marvelled at how calm he seemed, humming a tune to the music on the radio and carelessly smoking a cigarette.

They drove through unfamiliar streets and eventually stopped beside the railings of a park. "Over there," said George, pointing to a row of houses opposite. "The house with the blue door. Ring the bell twice and give the package to the man that answers it. Just that."

The distance from the house to the car was only a few hundred yards but to Candy it seemed like miles. She walked stiffly, not daring to look either to left or right. She reached out a trembling hand for the bell and pressed weakly, twice. Then a small man with glasses was standing there. He grabbed the package from her and banged the door in her face.

"Not too bad, was it?" said George, smiling at her as she got back into the car. "The boss will be pleased."

This time the journey was longer and they drove away from built-up city streets and out to suburbs where large houses lay half hidden behind high walls. Candy was reminded of Howth. George parked under a tree and pointed to an opening in a wall and steps leading down to a river bank.

"Now this one's a bit different. Go down those steps. There's a seat at the bottom. Sit there. A woman will come and sit beside you and say, 'It's a shame. All the fish in the river have been killed by pollution.' When she says that you start counting to a hundred. When you've reached a hundred just get up and walk away, leaving the package on the seat behind you. Now Candy, have you got all that?"

Candy nodded.

"If someone sits down and says nothing, then the plan is off. You just get up and leave and take the package with you. Okay—off you go. And try and look a bit more cheerful. You have to be a bit of an actress for this job."

This time she felt less nervous. She was glad that she didn't have to knock on anyone's door. She walked cheerfully down the steps and out of sight of the car. The seat was there, just as George had described it. She sat down and waited.

At first she didn't worry when nobody came, reasoning that the woman could have been delayed. Then she began to sense that something was wrong as she heard, or imagined she heard rustlings in the bushes behind her.

She must have been there at least ten minutes—her contact would never have been this late. Why hadn't George come to find out what was happening? She stood up, putting the package down on the seat. Then she changed her mind and retrieved it, realizing that she would be blamed if the drugs were lost. She turned towards the steps, intending

to make her way back to George when—
"Gotcha!"

The bushes behind her parted and she was surrounded by people. She was grabbed by both arms and frog-marched towards the steps.

"Now my girl," said one of the men, taking the package from her hand. "You've got a lot of explaining to do. You had better come along with us, we've a few questions we'd like you to answer."

Up on the road there was no sign of George's car. Candy, too frightened to think, never mind to act, allowed herself to be bundled into the back of a blue car. A man and a woman sat on either side of her and another couple sat in the front.

In silence they drove through the suburbs that Candy had passed by only half an hour ago.

She closed her eyes and listened in horror as the driver began to speak into a walkie talkie. She was in a police car and these were police men and women. George must have seen what was happening and at this very moment was on his way back to report to the man. And once he knew, Sharon's life would be in danger. At all costs Candy knew she must keep her mouth closed, tell them absolutely nothing. That was her only hope of saving Sharon.

In the barracks she was taken into a room furnished with armchairs and a coffee table. It wasn't a bit like the interrogation centres Candy had seen on television programmes.

A motherly woman came over to her and said, "Sure you're only a baby. Would you like some orange juice or a glass of milk?"

"No, thank you."

The woman looked at her. "What's your name, love?"

"Can—Charlie."

The woman looked at her again. "And where do you come from, Charlie?"

But Candy's lips were sealed.

They questioned her for hours, the woman and one of the men who had arrested her, taking it in turns. Sometimes they were cross and shouting and then they would become friendly and try to wheedle information out of her. Candy sat staring in front of her, refusing all food and drink.

She tried to block out their voices and she kept on repeating to herself, "I must say nothing, I must say nothing. Sharon's life depends on my silence."

By evening however she could stand it no

longer. "Please," she appealed to her two
tormentors, "please may I just have some
sleep?"

Instead of replying, the woman suddenly
jumped up. "That's it!" She snapped her
fingers. "I've got it. I knew I'd seen that face
before. It's been troubling me all day." She
swung round to Candy. "Well Charlie—you're
Candida O'Brien, aren't you, the missing
child? You've had you hair cut, that and trying
to pass yourself off as a boy put me off at first.
Well Candida—I'm right, aren't I?"

Candy burst into tears.

They left her alone then, closing the door
and rushing off. Candy was overwhelmed with
a sense of failure, a feeling that she had let
Sharon down. Now that they knew who she
was they would worm the rest of the
information out of her. Even at this stage they
might know that she and Sharon had run
away together. Where was Sharon? What
awful things might the man be doing to her?
She remembered his knife, she imagined
brave little Sharon and Blackie. She—

The door was flung open and there stood Mr
and Mrs O'Brien. Candy ran to them and they
put their arms round her. For some moments
none of them could speak and Candy didn't

want to, so overjoyed was she to be re-united with her parents. It was only when her father said, "And now we're taking you home. I've never heard such nonsense as you being involved in drug pushing," that she suddenly remembered the full horror of her situation.

"Darling," her mother said, seeing her daughter's expression. "What is it? You mustn't worry, Candy, whatever's happened. We've found you now and that's all that matters."

Could she trust her parents? She had to. On her own she would never be able to rescue Sharon but maybe her parents could come up with some plan.

When she told them, Mrs O'Brien took her in her arms again. "You poor darling—we should never have left you with that awful woman."

"Candy," her father took her hand. "We've got to tell the Gárdaí."

"No. No, no, no! If you do Sharon is as good as dead." She began to cry again, her sobs rising hysterically. "You don't know what he's like, how evil he is. He said, he *swore* he would kill us if—"

"Candy, you have to be brave. Stay here with Mum and I'll be back soon."

In silence Candy and her mother waited. When she thought of that kitchen and Sharon and Blackie, Candy's stomach began to heave and she stuffed a handkerchief into her mouth, sure that she was going to be sick.

When her father returned he was accompanied by a tall policeman. "This is Sergeant McArthur, Candy. Now I want you to tell him exactly what you've told us. Don't be afraid. He has a good idea who these people are."

Now that Candy had to tell her story she did so quickly for she knew that every second counted if Sharon was going to be rescued.

"Yes," said Sergeant McArthur, "that sounds like the Black Baron and his side-kick, George O'Toole. And we shouldn't have any trouble finding the house. We know where Sharon's grandmother lives—she reported Sharon's disappearance to us."

Back in the police car once more but this time seated between her parents, Candy stared out at the passing streets.

"Now, it must be somewhere in this area," said Sergeant McArthur and the car began to cruise slowly. "As soon as you think you recognise any place, just let us know."

Suddenly Candy cried, "There it is!" She

was pointing across the road. "I'm sure that's it. I remember the boarded up windows and the weeds in the garden. If you stop the car I'll show you how to get in round the back."

"Not so fast, young lady," Sergeant McArthur put a restraining hand on her arm. "From now on this is a matter for the Gárdaí. You can watch with your parents if you want to—so long as you stay well back."

The car drove to the end of the street where it stopped. Soon two other police cars joined it. Quietly men began to emerge from the cars and stealthily they made a ring around the house. When they were all in place Sergeant McArthur stepped forward with a loudhailer in his hand. Candy and her parents watched from the opposite corner where they had crouched down behind a tree.

"Baron and George O'Toole," the sergeant's voice came out loud and slightly distorted. "We know you're inside and we know you've got Sharon Dempsey with you. Let the girl out first and then you two come out with your hands in the air. The house is surrounded so you might as well be sensible."

When he had stopped speaking the silence seemed enormous. Everyone in the street was listening intently but there was nothing to hear.

"Come on now, Baron, be sensible. Why make things more difficult for yourself. Let the girl go."

Again silence filled the street.

Candy felt she could stand it no longer. Suddenly she broke from her parents' grasp and began to run, swift as a hare towards the house. Zig-zagging, she escaped several outstretched blue arms and was around the back of the house, heading for the secret entrance. She didn't care now what happened to her, all she knew was that she must get Sharon out.

She was at the window when, great joy, she heard a dog bark. Before anyone could stop her she was pounding on the boards. "Blackie, Sharon, it's me."

And faintly but distinctly came Sharon's reply, "You took your time."

11

Blood Sisters Forever

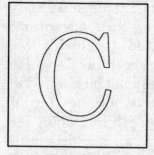andy was back in her bedroom in Howth, under the eaves, looking down at the sea. It was different now though for it contained twin beds and rather a lot of clothes thrown around. Tidiness was not one of Sharon's virtues.

It was three months since the day of Sharon's rescue and a very great deal had happened.

The Baron and George had been arrested, mainly because Candy had been able to tell the Gárdaí the registration number of George's car. They had been intercepted at Rosslare where they had been waiting to escape on the ferry to Fishguard. Now they were both in jail, serving long sentences.

Sharon had been re-united with her granny and sisters, and with her father the next day.

He had found work in London but no accommodation for five daughters who would have to remain with their grandmother.

However, as the grandmother was so old and her flat so small and as Sharon and Candy had become so close during their adventure, Mr and Mrs O'Brien had persuaded Mr Dempsey to allow them to keep his daughter as a foster child. They would not be allowed to adopt her for as soon as he found accommodation or another job in Dublin Mr Dempsey intended to have all his girls with him once more.

Sharon spent every Sunday with her granny and Candy usually went too. By now they were well used to the journey on the DART. Candy was overjoyed to have her blood sister living with her and was looking forward to introducing her at school in a week's time.

There was another addition to the O'Brien family. Blackie now lived in an elegant dog basket in the kitchen. It had taken some time before Pangur Bán would accept the newcomer but once he realized that Blackie would not replace him on Candy's bed at night, they had become friends, even though Pangur secretly thought that Blackie was a bit of a mutt.

"Hey, Sharon." Candy looked over at her blood sister.

"Yeh?"

"I was just wondering—are you happy living here?"

"I love it," Sharon smiled. "Sometimes I get lonely for my Da but I know we'll all be together again some day. It's ace being here with you, Candy."

Later that evening, as the family was finishing their meal, Candy suddenly asked, "By the way, did you ever find the Yeti?"

Her father shook his head. "Not exactly. I mean we didn't actually get a photograph of it or see it properly. But one morning I was up very early and I saw a giant shadow on a peak just above me—I'm sure it was the Yeti. We're going to have to organize another expedition and go back there."

The girls looked at one another and Mrs O'Brien laughed. "You should see the expression on your faces! Sharon, do you think your father would have any objection to your going on a trip to the Himalayas?"

"Mum—you don't mean—"

"Mrs O'Brien, you can't—"

"I think we should get you girls in training. Conditions will be perfect in about nine months time and that would give you plenty of time to get really fit. You wouldn't be able to do the whole climb but I don't see why you couldn't come as far as base camp with us."

Mr O'Brien laughed. "It would be safer than leaving you with Mrs Nolan."

Candy thought of white peaks and pure mountain air and remembered all the stories she had listened to and read since she was a toddler. Sharon just thought about shaking hands with the Yeti.

"Now don't get over excited," said Mrs O'Brien. "But you two have proved your worth in a sticky situation. I think you'd be a great help on an expedition."

"Ace," breathed Candy with shining eyes.

"Super ace," said Sharon.

And they shook hands across the table like true blood sisters.